To Fern and Sophia—R.W.

To Ian and William—C.J.C.

Hungry Hen
Text copyright © 2001 by Richard Waring
Illustrations copyright © 2001 by Caroline Jayne Church
Printed in Hong Kong. All rights reserved.
www.harperchildrens.com

Library of Congress Cataloging-in-Publication Data
Waring, Richard (Richard M. N.)
Hungry hen / by Richard Waring ; illustrated by Caroline Jayne Church.
p. cm.
Summary: A greedy fox watches a hungry hen growing bigger every day, knowing that the longer he waits to eat her, the bigger she will be.
ISBN 0-06-623880-3
[1. Chickens—Fiction. 2. Foxes—Fiction.] I. Church, Caroline, ill. II. Title.
PZ7.W2356 Hu 2002   2001024044
[E]—dc21   CIP
                                                                 AC

Typography by Al Cetta
1 2 3 4 5 6 7 8 9 10

❖

First HarperCollins Edition, 2001
Originally published by Oxford University Press, England, 2001

HUNGRY HEN

Richard Waring

Illustrated by
Caroline Jayne Church

HarperCollinsPublishers

There once was a very hungry little hen,
and she ate and ate, and grew and grew,
and the more she ate, the more she grew.

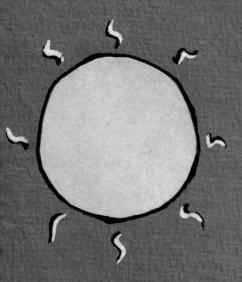

Up on the hill lived a fox.
Every morning the fox stared
down at the farm, and the hen
would come out of her house
looking bigger than ever.

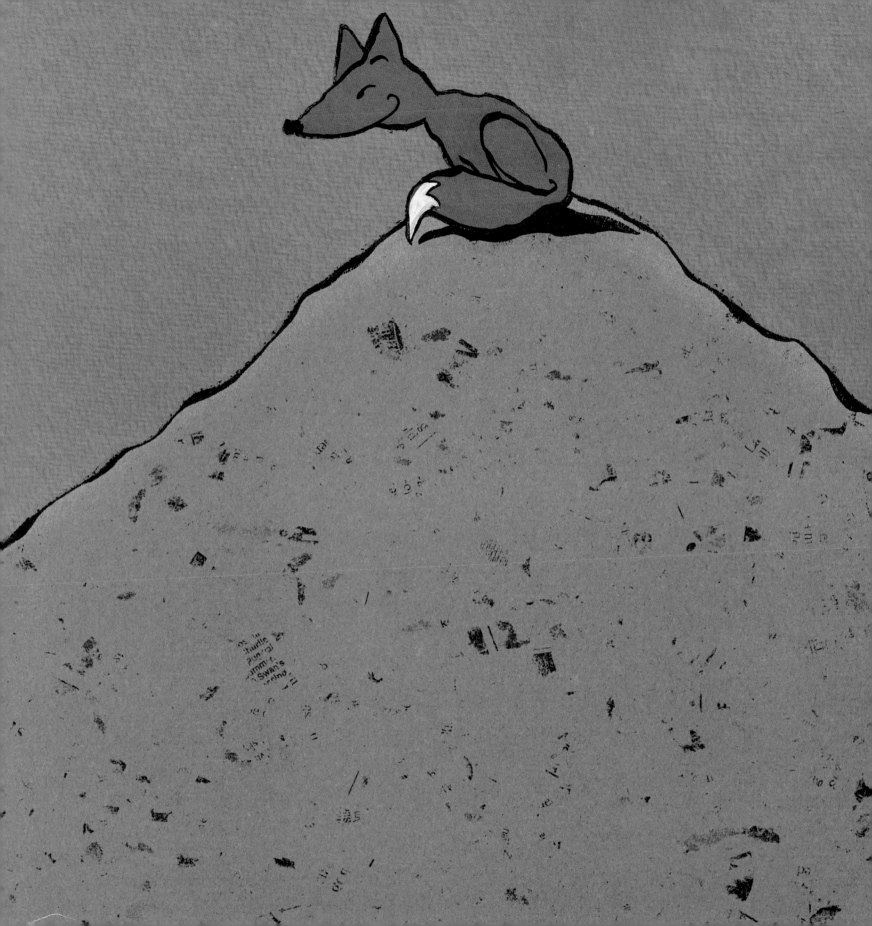

But every morning, as the fox
began to sneak down toward
the farm, he would stop and
think, "If I wait just one more
day, the hen will be even bigger."

And so he waited and waited and waited,
and the hen grew bigger and bigger,

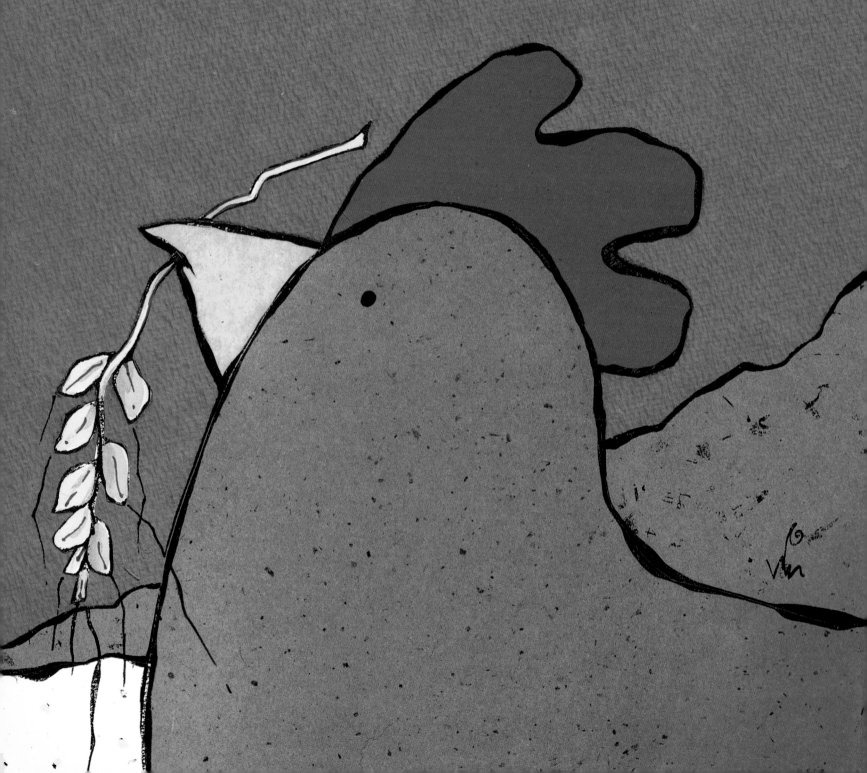

and the fox grew hungrier and hungrier,
and thinner and thinner.

Until one day, the fox looked down at the farm, and all he could see was the hen's enormous head squeezing through the door of her house.

The fox could stand it no longer.
He began to run.
He ran, and ran.

He ran faster and faster,
straight down the hill,
through the farm,

and *crashed*
through the window,
into the hen's house.

The fox looked at the hen.

The hen looked at the fox.

The fox licked his lips.

And just as the fox

was about

to pounce....

the hen bent down—
and gobbled him all up!